Simon the Cat

The Adventures of a Very Special Kitty

Margaret Rose Erickson

Tellwell Talent
www.tellwell.ca

ISBN
978-1-77302-230-7 (Paperback)

Simon's Signature Page

*I hope you enjoy reading about
my rescue and my new home.*

*I have had many adventures since
I was adopted and I will soon be
paw-printing more of them.*

— SIMON THE CAT

This book is dedicated to the memory of my sisters,

Mildred and Ruth

Their kindness to animals and to everyone they knew

will be remembered always

Preface

These are the first and second stories in a series of books written about Simon the Cat

All writings are, for the most part, based on the true adventures and happenings in the life of Simon the Cat.

Once upon a time, Simon was a homeless kitty, cared for by the Humane Society in Phoenix, Arizona. He was very ill with an upper respiratory infection and was brought back to health by the wonderful care of the animal hospital, operated by the Humane Society.

He was adopted by the author of this story and her husband and each year he spends six months in Canada and six months in the United States – he has travelled thousands of miles and enjoys his home in Canada and in Arizona – a true dual citizen.

He has proved over and over again what a devoted, grateful kitty he is. He is indeed loving – and he is indeed loved.

A percentage of the profit from the sale of Simon's books will be donated to the Humane Societies in both Canada and the U.S.

— Margaret Rose Erickson

THE RESCUE

Simon was a big white kitty with lovely green eyes and pretty grey designs on his furry coat. He lived in a big blue house with many people and lots of other cats and dogs.

One day the people sold their big blue house and moved to a city far, far away. They left Simon behind – all alone – to look after himself.

'Oh, what am I going to do?" - cried Simon - "I am all alone and I am so very hungry and very cold. Oh how I wish I had a nice warm house to live in and a Mommy and Daddy to look after me."

Simon started to shiver. "I have never been so hungry and cold and I'm also a little bit scared," he thought.

Simon trudged along, looking into the windows of houses, seeing families together. He became colder and colder and started to cough. Tears trickled down Simon's green eyes but he quickly wiped them away and tried to look brave as he continued to trudge along - but - his cough was getting worse.

Suddenly Simon saw a lovely little house and through the window he saw a mother and father and children and a kitty. The pretty young girl was petting the kitty.

"Oh!" said Simon, "There's a Mommy and Daddy – look how they are petting a kitty just like me! Maybe if I tap on the window they will let me in."

A kind lady came to the door, looked around the corner, and saw Simon.

"Oh you poor kitty! You look hungry! Stay there and I will bring you something to eat and drink."

The lady sat a dish of food and a dish of water on the front steps and Simon ran toward it and quickly started to eat, but he had trouble eating since his cough was getting worse.

"Oh this is so good," - thinks Simon. "I don't know when I have ever had such a yummy dinner. I wonder if they want another kitty to live with them?"

The kind lady came back out to where Simon was hungrily eating his dinner. She smiled kindly at him, pet his head, and said,

"There, now that you have had a nice dinner, you must be on your way. We have a kitty of our own and there just isn't room for you here."

The lady goes back inside the house and closes the door.

Simon walks slowly away and can hardly wipe away all the tears in his sad, green eyes. He starts coughing very hard.

"Oh I wish I could have a home like that, with a Mommy and Daddy of my own. Tonight when I say my prayers I will ask for just that."

As Simon is walking away, he hears the kind lady in the house say,

"I think I will call the Humane Society – they will know what to do with a little homeless kitty."

As Simon is trudging along, coughing, he sees a pretty van drive by. The van has pictures of happy kitties and dogs all over it. A very friendly, jolly man stops the van, jumps out, picks Simon up and puts him on a cuddly blanket in the van.

"There, there my fine fellow," he says - "We will soon have you in a nice warm place where you will be fed and a doctor will check up on that bad cough you have – you are certainly a handsome kitty!!!"

They drive up to a pretty building called "The Humane Society – A Home For Homeless Animals" and next to it is another building called "The Humane Society's Hospital," where the driver takes Simon.

A doctor rushes over to Simon and examines him and says, "Hello my fine kitty, my name is Doctor Kelly and I am a veterinarian. I can see you have a very bad cold my boy, and we have just the medicine to make you feel better. You will be as fit as a fiddle in a day or two – lucky you came to us when you did! You are very ill but you will soon be better and as good as new."

Doctor Kelly tells him,

"Tomorrow, if you are feeling better, you can go to a special room to play and have your very own bed. I see on your collar that your name is Simon. So, Simon my boy, here at the Humane Society people come by to adopt kitties. Perhaps you will be adopted and go to your very own home. I know you would like that."

Simon is all snuggled up in a kitty bed and blankets and he thinks,

"Oh I am so warm and comfy – and maybe, just maybe, a Mommy and Daddy will come to get me soon. I would love that."

Simon woke up the next morning with a big stretch and a full tummy. Doctor Kelly said to him, "Good morning Simon! It looks like you are feeling much better and your cough is almost gone."

"I have some news for you. Right after breakfast you are going over to the playroom next door. That is where kitties stay and play – and where they can be adopted!"

What Simon the Cat did not know was that a big surprise was waiting for him – and that soon all his wishes would come true.

Simon Gets A New Home

Simon is jumping up and down – he is so excited he can hardly eat his breakfast. He thinks -

"Oh my goodness! Oh my goodness! What if there is a Mommy and Daddy over there? Will they like me? Will they want a white and grey kitty? Oh my goodness! Will they think I am too little – or too big? Oh my goodness! Will they think I am the wrong color? If there is a Mommy and Daddy there who want to adopt a kitty, please, please make them want me!"

A friendly nurse picks Simon up and takes him from the hospital over to the Humane Society's playroom that is just for kitties. In the playroom there are lots of toys, a climbing tree, kitty beds and wonderful pictures on the wall of happy little kitties. Simon looks at all the pretty things, his eyes as big as saucers.

Simon looks over at the sofa in the corner of the playroom where there is a man and lady. The lady says to Simon,

"My what a lovely kitty you are. Would it be alright if I picked you up and put you on my knee?"

Simon thinks, - "Oh, yes, yes, yes, please pick me up! I want to snuggle and would love for you to pet me – I will be a good kitty and I know how to purr!"

The lady holds Simon on her knee, pets him, and then passes him to her husband to cuddle. He says,

"Now this is what I would call one fine kitty. Simon, there is something I would like you to know – an adopted kitty is a very, very special kitty and you are very special. I think you should come home to live with us. What do you think?"

Simon is so happy that he starts to cry happy tears – he cannot stop smiling and purring. He is so, so happy and he thinks,

"I am so happy I am crying – now isn't that silly! I can't believe I am going to have my very own home and a Mommy and Daddy – my prayers have been answered!"

Simon's new Mommy and Daddy take him to the pet store where they buy him a blanket, toys, food and a basket full of wonderful kitty things. Simon looks at everything with huge eyes, thinking,

"I can't believe this is all for me - oh, oh, oh - I'm starting to cry those happy tears again. I think I am the happiest and luckiest kitty in the whole wide world!"

Simon's new Mommy and Daddy take him to their big white truck and settle him into the back seat on some comfy blankets for the drive home.

Simon looks out the window and sees such wonderful sights - the Arizona desert with pretty cactuses blooming, huge saguaros and lots of roadrunners scampering along. Simon laughs at the roadrunners and sends them a happy "meow!".

They drive up to a house and Simon's Mommy says,

"Simon, this is your new home! You can look around if you like."

Simon looks out through patio doors and sees a wonderful yard with water fountains – birds are even drinking in the fountain. There is a little bridge and beyond that, a golf course with golfers going by, who wave at him.

"Oh, this is so pretty," thinks Simon. "I could just sit here and look at all of this forever."

Simon's Mommy says,

"Simon, here's your food and water dish, eat up now sweetheart, as you have had a very busy day. Then it will be time for bed."

Simon eats his food and has a drink of water, but just can't stop purring because he is so happy and content. His Mommy and Daddy go to their room and go to bed. Simon goes to his room and thinks,

"This is a lovely room and I love my little kitty bed, but already I am missing my Mommy and Daddy. I think I will go to their room."

Simon walks softly into his Mommy and Daddy's room and quietly jumps up onto their bed.

His Mommy says, "Simon, you sweet little kitty – you want to sleep with us! That is quite alright. You just curl up here in the middle and we will snuggle and cuddle you until you go to sleep."

Simon thinks,

"I know I am the happiest kitty that ever could be – I love my Mommy and Daddy. I love my new home and now I am going to sleep."

What Simon doesn't know is that his adventures are just beginning...

MARGARET, BRUCE AND SIMON ERICKSON

Bruce, Margaret and Simon live in Ponoka, Alberta, Canada. Prior to retirement, they operated a John Deere Farm Equipment business in Ponoka.

They reside in Ponoka during the summer months and at Robson Ranch in Eloy, Arizona during the winter months.

Simon the Cat loves both countries.

THE FOLLOWING PAGES ARE REAL PICTURES OF SIMON THE CAT

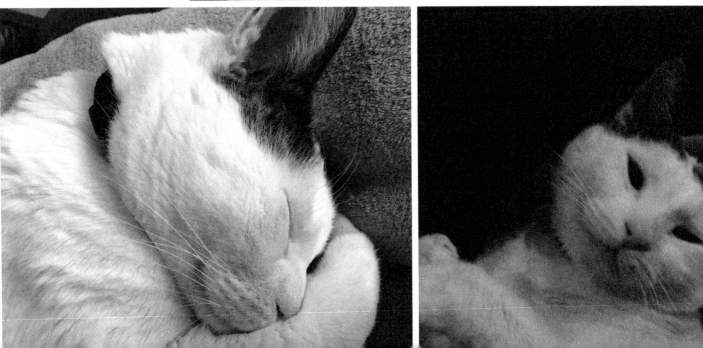

CHRISTMAS TIME

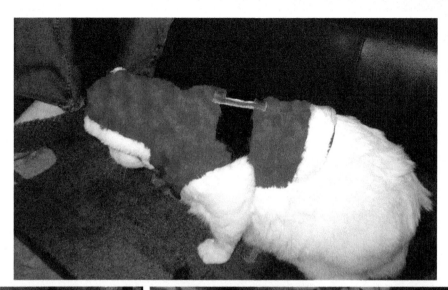

SIMON LOVES JOHN DEERE

RELAXING

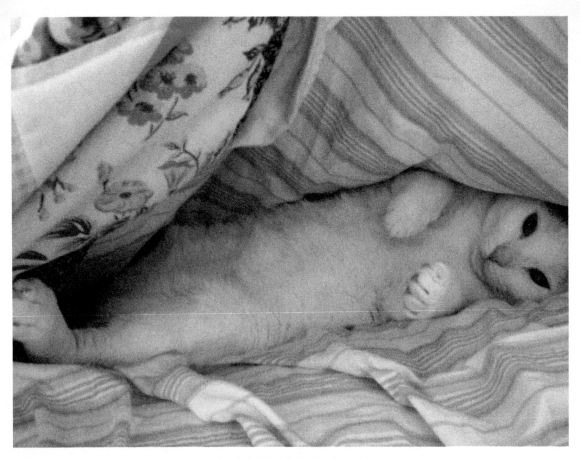

IS IT TIME TO GET UP?

I THINK I HAVE OUTGROWN MY KITTY CASTLE

I'M JUST TOO TIRED TO EAT

SIMON'S FRIEND, MAC THE DOG, VISITS
SIMON'S OUTDOOR PLAYROOM

SIMON'S FRIEND, SQUEAKY THE SQUIRREL,
VISITS SIMON'S OUTDOOR PLAYROOM

05/18/2006

*HURRY – TAKE THE PICTURE, I CAN'T
HOLD THIS POSE MUCH LONGER*

I LOVE TO HELP MOMMY TYPE

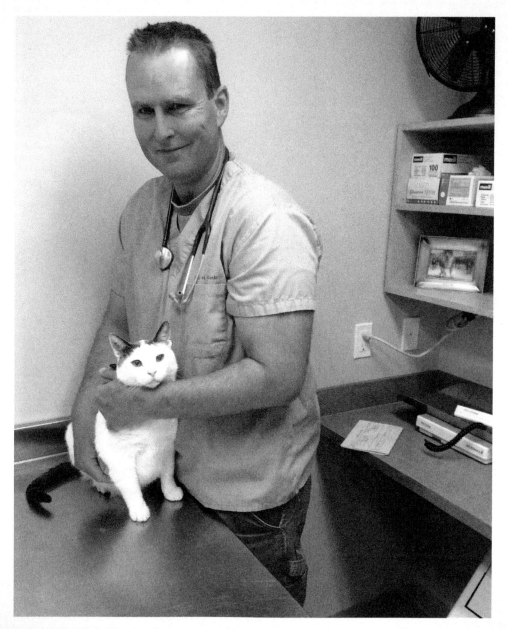

SIMON AND DOCTOR KELLY

SIMON SUPERVISES THE MANUSCRIPT OF
"SIMON THE CAT"

CPSIA information can be obtained
at www.ICGtesting.com
Printed in the USA
BVOW10s1429111216

470458BV00011B/49/P